Acting Edition

The Complete Works of Jane Austen, Abridged

by Jessica Bedford,
Kathryn MacMillan,
Charlotte Northeast, and
Meghan Winch

This work is published by Samuel French, an imprint of Concord Theatricals Corp.

No one shall make any changes in this title(s) for the purpose of production. No part of this book may be reproduced, stored in a retrieval system, scanned, uploaded, or transmitted in any form, by any means, now known or yet to be invented, including mechanical, electronic, digital, photocopying, recording, videotaping, or otherwise, without the prior written permission of the publisher. No one shall share this title(s), or any part of this title(s), through any social media or file hosting websites.

For all inquiries regarding motion picture, television, online/digital and other media rights, please contact Concord Theatricals Corp.

MUSIC AND THIRD-PARTY MATERIALS USE NOTE

Licensees are solely responsible for obtaining formal written permission from copyright owners to use copyrighted music and/or other copyrighted third-party materials (e.g. artworks, logos) in the performance of this play and are strongly cautioned to do so. If no such permission is obtained by the licensee, then the licensee must use only original music and materials that the licensee owns and controls. Licensees are solely responsible and liable for clearances of all third-party copyrighted materials, including without limitation music, and shall indemnify the copyright owners of the play(s) and their licensing agent, Concord Theatricals Corp., against any costs, expenses, losses and liabilities arising from the use of such copyrighted third-party materials by licensees. For music, please contact the appropriate music licensing authority in your territory for the rights to any incidental music.

IMPORTANT BILLING AND CREDIT REQUIREMENTS

If you have obtained performance rights to this title, please refer to your licensing agreement for important billing and credit requirements.

THE COMPLETE WORKS OF JANE AUSTEN, ABRIDGED premiered at The Physick House in Philadelphia, PA, on May 29, 2019, produced by Tiny Dynamite. It was directed by Kathryn MacMillan, the scenic and props designer was Sara Outing, the costume designer was Janus Stefanowicz, the sound designer and composer was Daniel Ison, the lighting designer was Michael Lambui, and the production stage manager was Kat Kelly. Minor revisions to the script allowed for a second sold-out run October 30–November 10, 2019. Performances once again took place at The Physick House and featured the same director and cast. The cast was as follows:

JESSICA . . . . Jessica Bedford

CHARLOTTE . . . . Charlotte Northeast

TREVOR. . . . . Trevor Fayle

THE COMPLETE WORKS OF JANE AUSTEN, ABRIDGED was developed through a series of group meetings (over wine and cheese) interspersed with solo writings by the Authors starting in the Summer of 2018. It received one in-house reading prior to the beginning of rehearsal in May of 2019 (during which it underwent further revision).

CHARACTERS

(names may be changed to those of the performers if desired.)

JESSICA who plays:

From *P&P*:	Jane Bennet
	Kitty Bennet
	Mr. Bingley
From *Emma*:	Emma Woodhouse
	Harriet Smith
From *Lady Susan*:	Lady Susan
From *S&S*:	Marianne Dashwood
	Fanny Dashwood
	Lucy Steele

CHARLOTTE (a/k/a **"CHUCK"**) who plays:

From *P&P*:	Lizzy Bennet
	Mary Bennet
	Lydia Bennet
	Mr. Collins
From *Emma*:	Mr. Elton
	Mrs. Weston
	Miss Bates (sort of)
From *S&S*:	Elinor Dashwood
	John Dashwood

TREVOR (a/k/a **"HARRY"**) who plays:

From *P&P*:	Mr. Bennet
	Mr. Darcy
	Mr. Wickham
	Lady Catherine de Bourgh
From *Emma*:	Mr. Knightley
From *Sanditon*:	Mr. Parker
From *S&S*:	Mr. Dashwood (father)
	Edward Ferrars
	John Willoughby
	Colonel Brandon

SETTING

The setting is an historic home. Or anything, really – an open room will do. But if you can find one with history and some sense of middle-class comforts (or make one on your stage), that's ideal.

TIME

The time is right now

AUTHORS' NOTES

A Note on Style:
If the three characters were a symphony, Jessica would play the lilting high notes, Charlotte would provide the steady, driving alto, and Trevor would be the dependable baritone – except when he's the excitable tenor.

While the styles of each individual section change (Game Show! Jewelbox Theater! Dramatic Trailer Voice!), what runs through all of it is quick-paced, high-spirited enthusiasm. Jessica, Charlotte, and (eventually) Trevor love Jane Austen, love her work, and are so very, very excited to share it with each other and the audience – irreverently, and without preciousness. They are equally enthusiastic and quick-on-their-feet about fully embracing (and nailing) the individual styles and frames they've chosen for each story – as well as the genuine feeling, when called for.

...	indicates trailing off
–	indicates being cut off by the next line
/	indicates overlapping text

A pause is longer than a beat.

There are a few references to locations in and around Philadelphia, as well as to the original production's runtime and set. Those are [bracketed] in the script; like the character names, bracketed text may be modified to fit the production.

"Welsh pudding" is a fabrication of the authors and means "super-hottie" in Jessica's world.

Scene One

*(**JESSICA** is lounging alone onstage, reading. **CHARLOTTE** enters. Looks around. **JESSICA** is absorbed in her book.)*

CHARLOTTE. Where's Harry?

JESSICA. Who?

CHARLOTTE. Harry. Harry Smith?

JESSICA. ...

CHARLOTTE. British actor? Our friend? *(Indicating a show program.)* He's in *The Complete Works of Jane Austen, Abridged*...our play...happening...now?

JESSICA. Oh, that guy. He's gone.

CHARLOTTE. Gone?

What do you mean gone?

JESSICA. He booked a gig in New York. A six-month contract, three shows in rep or something... *(Returns to her book.)*

CHARLOTTE. But. What do we do? He was going to be all the men!

JESSICA. *(Still reading.)* I'm not worried about it. A solution will present itself. Meanwhile, I'll keep working.

CHARLOTTE. Respectfully, Jessica. It doesn't look like you're working.

JESSICA. I'm rereading *Pride and Prejudice*. *(Philosophically.)* I'm turning the page to a new world.

CHARLOTTE. But we need to solve this Harry crisis!

JESSICA. Just as soon as I finish this chapter. *(Turns another page.)* Oh, look! Another chapter!

(Continues reading.)

CHARLOTTE. People are here!

JESSICA. Hi!

CHARLOTTE. We have to do something!

JESSICA. *(Reading from her book.)* My courage always rises at every attempt to intimidate me.

CHARLOTTE. *(Working it out on her own.)* Okay, so we'll just have to recast the role. Roles. Jane Austen's men are all so different. Darcy: the romantic hero. Bingley: an excitable puppy. Knightley, a bit of a noodge. Wickham: charming but rakish. Willoughby: charming but rakish. Frank Churchill: charming but rakish. *(With some hope.)* There's a theme emerging there anyway.

*(**TREVOR** enters, in full Regency splendor.)*

JESSICA. *(Looking up from her book, not without thirst.)* Oh, hello.

CHARLOTTE. *(To **TREVOR**.)* We're about to start. Late seating is in the back. *(Motions for him to sit; he doesn't.)* Enjoy the show.

*(To **JESSICA**.)* We don't have a show.

TREVOR. *(Tugs at his waistcoat or something.)* I read in *Playbill* that you might be looking for a third performer?

JESSICA. We didn't post the gig in *Playbill*.

CHARLOTTE. Yeah, I didn't even know we had lost an actor until like two minutes ago.

TREVOR. I saw Harry's name in a cast listing for a show running in New York. And I knew you had this show running here, so I took a chance that you might be looking for a replacement. I'm Trevor. I'm a huge Jane Austen fan?

CHARLOTTE. Is that right.

TREVOR. Yep. Yes? Yeah. I am. *(Beat.)* Okay, I only sort of know Jane Austen. But I needed the gig. Also, I feel awesome in this costume. I'm dashing!

JESSICA. What do you think, Chuck?

CHARLOTTE. What else are we going to do? The audience is here. You're in. One condition. I'm still going to call you Harry. I'm an actress of a certain age so I only have so much bandwidth.

TREVOR. Harry it is. *(Beams.)*

JESSICA. Men. All they gotta do is show up.

CHARLOTTE. Yeah. Some of us have to write our own material to make sure we get cast.

> (**CHARLOTTE** *and* **JESSICA** *take to the audience; then exeunt.)*

Scene Two

(**JESSICA** *re-enters, followed by* **CHARLOTTE.** *They are mid-argument.*)

CHARLOTTE. You're a populist!

JESSICA. And you're a snob! Or a contrarian! Or a contrary snob!

CHARLOTTE. That's a horrible thing to say to me.

JESSICA. I'm sorry. I only mostly meant it.

TREVOR. *(Entering.)* Um...what seems to be the problem?

CHARLOTTE. Oh, not much. Except the same argument we've been having for years.

JESSICA. It doesn't have to be. Just admit that *Pride and Prejudice* is better than *Persuasion* and it's all done. Like a flu shot. One little prick to your tiny ego and we're good to go.

CHARLOTTE. Admit that *Pride and Prejudice* is better than *Persuasion*? Never. It would be a lie.

JESSICA. Anne Elliot is more changeable than my underpants.

TREVOR. *(Quickly, almost as an aside.)* Who?

CHARLOTTE. Lizzy Bennet is an over-indulged teenager.

TREVOR. Who?

CHARLOTTE. Anne Elliot thinks before she speaks.

JESSICA. Then she's an awfully slow thinker! When does she finally open her mouth? Chapter thirty?!

CHARLOTTE. *(In a low how-dare-you grumbly growl.)* It's a novella and you know that.

JESSICA. Lizzy Bennett is quick witted and sharp.

CHARLOTTE. Lizzy Bennett is snarky and unfair.

JESSICA. *(In a low how-dare-you grumbly growl.)* That's the whole point of the story.

She learns her lesson!

CHARLOTTE. She's rewarded for bad behavior. But *Persuasion* is a love story for grown-ups!

JESSICA. Which means it's boring!

TREVOR. I'm a little lost…

CHARLOTTE. Excuse you. We're in the middle of an argument. This is about the core of our souls, our *weltanschauungs* on humanity, what defines decency –

JESSICA. Which book is better – *Pride and Prejudice* or *Persuasion.*

TREVOR. Great titles.

JESSICA. Right?

TREVOR. So, which one IS better? I don't know them…well.

CHARLOTTE. Neither of them?

TREVOR. Nope.

JESSICA. How about *Sense and Sensibility*?

TREVOR. Uh…no.

CHARLOTTE. *Emma?*

TREVOR. I don't think so.

JESSICA. So, if you don't know the arguably big hitters, I'm gonna guess you don't know *Lady Susan, Mansfield Park, Northanger Abbey* –

TREVOR. Oh, I know that last one! My mom lost it over the Christmas special, where Matthew proposed to Lady Mary.

JESSICA. That's *Downton Abbey*. And that scene was amazing.

CHARLOTTE. You have the attention span of a goldfish.

JESSICA. Thank you.

CHARLOTTE. It wasn't a compliment! We have a major problem here.

JESSICA. We do?

CHARLOTTE. This is *The Complete Works of Jane Austen* and the guy we just hired doesn't know ANYTHING.

(*Re: the audience.*) These people paid money for this.

JESSICA. (*Looking at the audience judgmentally.*) You did? How much?

TREVOR. Hey, look, it's not that big of a deal, right? C'mon, we can sort this out.

(*Beat.*)

Please, I really need this gig.

JESSICA. Harry can learn on the job. (*To audience, raising her hand.*) Anyone here not a Jane Austen superfan? (*Encourage and vamp as needed as there will likely be some folks with hands up. Then, to Chuck:*) See? Seems appropriate only two-thirds of us know the stories. Actually, I envy you. To get to discover Jane for the very first time? You're gonna love it.

CHARLOTTE. Okay. Fine. But we'll need to start from scratch. Let's just start with the basics, then. I mean the basic basics. Why is Austen so beloved today?

TREVOR. Okay, so I did a Wikipedia search, and she was a badass. A popular female voice during a time when patriarchy ruled deeply and ruthlessly. I mean, do we get into (*Scrolling on his phone.*) inheritance laws and land entails here?

CHARLOTTE. No, no. Let's keep this to first draft stuff. An outline.

TREVOR. Right. So. Not just a popular voice – a witty voice, a deeply intelligent voice.

CHARLOTTE. Good. This is good. What else?

TREVOR. *(Scrolling.)* Published six beloved novels: *Pride and Prejudice* –

JESSICA. SWOON.

CHARLOTTE. Ugh, not now, you. Continue.

TREVOR. *(Scrolling.)* Also *Sense and Sensibility*, *Northanger Abbey*, *Mansfield Park*, *Emma*, and *Persuasion*.

CHARLOTTE. Mmmm, *Persuasion* is –

JESSICA. Nooo, not now, you!

CHARLOTTE. Fine. And?

TREVOR. And?

CHARLOTTE. And?! Loads else! The wild juvenilia! The unfinished, what-could-have-been novels *Sanditon* and *The Watsons*! The savage *Lady Susan*, which she finished but left unpublished! A tantalizingly thin biography: one hundred and sixty-one letters, one brief and broken engagement, and an early death at forty-one!

(To **JESSICA.***)* Anything to add to that?

JESSICA. Great tits.

TREVOR. Excuse me?

CHARLOTTE. Are you saying Jane Austen had –

JESSICA. I don't know. Maybe, maybe not. That is *exactly* my point. She was writing when every woman had great tits.

(Off their looks.)

Dudes. Empire waists. Everyone had great tits. It was a great equalizing time for women. Plus, looser corsets so everyone could breathe. That's not small either. That's why her heroines were all so smart. Oxygen was actually able to circulate to their brains.

(Again.)

That's just science. That's not me.

CHARLOTTE. So, you're saying she's beloved because empire waists gave everyone great tits...

JESSICA. Okay. So, we picture ourselves as twin spirits to the protagonist, right? Austen writes in third person omniscient, so you think you're right there, right next to Elizabeth Bennet, like you're her best friend. You know more of her inner thoughts than Jane, her sister, does, than her best friend does. And you love her – Lizzy – because you see parts of yourself in her. Or at least you see the way you'd like to be manifested in her. And boom – you find yourself in a rainstorm under a gazebo with the unattainable Mr. Darcy –

CHARLOTTE. That's the Keira Knightley. That's not in the book.

JESSICA. Shh. You find yourself in a rainstorm under a gazebo with Darcy, and he's looking at you all obstinate and hot and you think, "Am I up for this moment?" and then you remember that you can actually breathe, and your tits look fabulous A.F. and you think, "Yes, yes – I can handle this moment. Bring it, you beautiful snob."

CHARLOTTE. Jane Austen and empire waists.

TREVOR. The confluence of two great things coming together at the same point in history.

CHARLOTTE. Galileo and the telescope.

TREVOR. Robert Hooke and the microscope.

JESSICA. Newton and gravity.

TREVOR. *(Slight beat.)* You do know that gravity pre-existed Newton…

JESSICA. Potato, potahto. Also, these dresses are half the reason her stories have been adapted into film. And half the reason people read the book is because they saw the movie first. People want to wear those clothes. It's not like the Victorian era – no one is dying to be Jane Eyre. Everyone wants to be Lizzy Bennet. No one looks good in Victorian clothes.

*(Looks at **CHARLOTTE**.)*

Except for maybe you. [You're tiny like Queen Vicky.] Look at your tiny feet!

CHARLOTTE. Let's get back to work, shall we? Her stories were contemporary to her time…

TREVOR. Yes?

CHARLOTTE. Great Britain was at war for the bulk of her adult life. And yet her novels never mention war.

JESSICA. No, but they mention soldiers! "I remember a time when I liked a red coat very much myself!"

CHARLOTTE. Yes, but. Her readers were a people at war, with the anxiety of war hanging over their heads. But in her stories, she gives them…life, in its greatest heights and banalities. One true love and muddy hems. She reminded them that life was still happening, would still happen despite the constant threat of calamity out there.

TREVOR. So, an empowered voice, a picture of lives thoroughly lived…

CHARLOTTE. And tits.

JESSICA. Amen.

Scene Three

TREVOR. OK then, where do we start with the storytelling part?

CHARLOTTE. The juvenilia?

TREVOR. Huh?

CHARLOTTE. All the stuff she wrote as a kid.

JESSICA. I think her younger writing is only fully appreciated in the context of her larger work. The contrast gives the reader a deeper appreciation of her emerging voice.

CHARLOTTE. That's...a good point.

JESSICA. So I vote we start with *Pride and Prejudice*.

*(This hurts **CHARLOTTE**'s soul.)*

It's her best-known work, Chuck. Deal with it.

CHARLOTTE. Fine.

JESSICA. To Hertfordshire, bitches!

CHARLOTTE. Oh god. We're gonna be here all day. The BBC *Pride and Prejudice* comes in, like, eight DVDs.

JESSICA. Six.

TREVOR. Including bonus features?

CHARLOTTE. Don't even ask.

JESSICA. I can tell it quick!

CHARLOTTE. How?

JESSICA. Silly hats and bonnets, of course!

(She has produced a collection of them, whether from backstage or hidden somewhere on the set.)

JESSICA. Okay, new kid, this is what you need to know. There's always a heroine. In our case it's Elizabeth Bennet or Lizzy or Eliza.

TREVOR. She has three names?

JESSICA. A name and nicknames. Just like how we sometimes call you Harry –

CHARLOTTE. And sometimes Trevor –

JESSICA. And sometimes Sweet Cheeks.

(Beat.)

TREVOR. When do you call me Sweet Cheeks?

JESSICA.	**CHARLOTTE.**
Don't worry about it.	Doesn't matter.

TREVOR. Okay. Elizabeth or Lizzy or Eliza.

CHARLOTTE. So, *Pride and Prejudice* starts, as everyone knows, at Longbourn, the Bennet family estate –

JESSICA. The family has five daughters.

TREVOR. Whoa.

CHARLOTTE. No birth control.

TREVOR. That's a lot of dowries.

CHARLOTTE. You ain't kidding.

JESSICA. There's Jane,

(Puts on Jane's hat.)

the eldest; she makes goodness a choice and she's a real slice of Welsh pudding if you know what I mean.

TREVOR. I do not.

JESSICA. *(As Jane.)* I would wish not to be hasty in censuring anyone but I always speak what I think. *(As herself.)* Then Lizzy. Our wit.

(**JESSICA** *offers Lizzy's hat to* **CHARLOTTE.**)

CHARLOTTE. What?

JESSICA. Here.

CHARLOTTE. Me?

JESSICA. Yes.

CHARLOTTE. Why?

JESSICA. PUT ON THE HAT.

CHARLOTTE. *(As Lizzy.)* There are few people whom I really love, and still fewer of whom I think well. The more I see of the world, the more am I dissatisfied with it; and every day confirms my belief of the inconsistency of all human characters, and of the little dependence that can be placed on the appearance of merit or sense.

JESSICA. Mary.

(Gives **CHARLOTTE** *glasses.)*

CHARLOTTE. *(As Mary. Clears throat.)* Vanity and pride –

JESSICA. Oh god. Please no. Lydia!

(Gives **CHARLOTTE** *a fan.)*

CHARLOTTE. *(As Lydia.)* Have you seen any pleasant men? Have you had any flirting?

(Beat. As herself.)

Wait. Didn't you forget about Kitty?

JESSICA. Who could blame me? Kitty!

(Dons hat, as Kitty.) But I am two years older. *(Cough cough cough.)*

(As herself.) We start with…

JESSICA & CHARLOTTE.   It is a truth universally acknowledged that a single man in possession of a good fortune must be in want of a wife.

CHARLOTTE. It's the most iconic line in all of Austen. I'll give it to *P&P* for that.

JESSICA. And it's the thesis of the novel. Introducing Mrs. Bennet.

*(Produces hat and gives it to **CHARLOTTE**.)*

She's…unhelpful.

And Mr. Bennet, a Patriarch. Though, one of the nice ones. I think our girl Jane Austen might've had some daddy issues.

*(Gives **TREVOR** a hat; he does not put it on.)*

CHARLOTTE. *(As Mrs. B.)* Mr. Bennet, Mr. Bennet, have you heard that Netherfield Park is let at last?

JESSICA. *(To **TREVOR**.)* Just be generally unhelpful.

TREVOR. *(As Mr. B. with a hat tucked under his arm, guessing.)* I had not.

JESSICA. Nailed it!

CHARLOTTE. *(As Mrs. B.)* But it is, for Mrs. Long has just been here, and she told me all about it. Do you not want to know who has taken it?

TREVOR. *(As Mr. B.)* *(Guessing, very contemporary.)* You want to tell me, and so that's fine I guess.

*(**CHARLOTTE** is rankled by the tone.)*

JESSICA. Close enough?

CHARLOTTE. *(As Mrs. B.)* Why, my dear, you must know, Mrs. Long says that Netherfield is taken by a young man of large fortune from the north of England; that he came down on Monday in a chaise and four to see the place, and was so much delighted with it –

TREVOR. Hang on. Hang on.

Is that how the story starts?

JESSICA. Yeah.

CHARLOTTE. What's your beef?

TREVOR. Isn't this an epochal feminist novel? And the goal is just to marry the women off?

JESSICA. Oh!

CHARLOTTE. Whoa!

JESSICA. No, no, no!

CHARLOTTE. This story is about so much more than finding a husband.

JESSICA. Preach!

CHARLOTTE. Her stories are about women finding themselves. We love the heroines because they are who they were on page one; their changes are about self-knowledge. They have the essential traits all along; it takes the challenge of a good partnership to help them realize it.

JESSICA. And what's astonishing about the happy couples at the end of her stories is that they are true partnerships – marriages of equals.

TREVOR. That's very modern.

CHARLOTTE. Or you could call it timeless.

JESSICA. Also, women's options were LIMITED. They couldn't work. In fact, in her lifetime, Austen's novels were published anonymously so as not to attach the stigma of a working woman to her family. Consequently, a woman was either a spinster and a financial burden to her male relatives, destitute, or she got married as a means of –

(Battle music.)*

Survival!

CHARLOTTE. Love is a battlefield.

JESSICA. *(To* **TREVOR.***)* So, first level of the game –

*(***CHARLOTTE** *does various battle poses and warmups.)*

we have to arrange to meet the guy. Profile on Charles Bingley –

(Holds up hat.)

New tenant at Netherfield. Incredibly affable, well off, and well liked. He's basically a human Labrador.

TREVOR. Let's go meet him!

JESSICA. No! Are you trying to get us socially killed?!

*(***CHARLOTTE** *acts out dodging a bullet.)*

A woman can't introduce herself to a man.

TREVOR. Seriously?

JESSICA. Fortunately, Papa Bennet comes through with an assist and calls on Bingley.

(To **TREVOR,** *who is still holding the hat.)* Be mildly helpful.

TREVOR. *(As Mr. B. Still super contemporary;* **JESSICA** *holds Bingley's hat.)* Hi. I have five daughters. Want to meet them?

CHARLOTTE. Dude, this is Regency England, not Saturday in [Fishtown].

---

* A license to produce *The Complete Works of Jane Austen, Abridged* does not include a performance license for any third-party or copyrighted recordings. Licensees should create their own.

TREVOR. Too casual?

JESSICA. A bit. Sometimes you need the costume. See if this helps your vibe!

> *(Puts Mr. B's hat on* **TREVOR.***)*

TREVOR. *(As Mr. B, in full.)* I will...assure him of my hearty consent to his marrying whichever he chooses of the girls.

TREVOR.	**CHARLOTTE.**	**JESSICA.**
Huh?	Whaaat?!	Woah!

JESSICA. Way better. Moving on! Bingley returns the call and meets the Bennet girls.

> *(We hear a riff of a song that's spunky and celebrates women*, while* **CHARLOTTE** *curtsies once.*

TREVOR. We met him! Now what?

> *(***CHARLOTTE** *-as-Lizzy again does something battle-like.)*

JESSICA. The gladiatorial ring of mating rituals –

TREVOR. Oh no...

JESSICA. The dance floor! The Meryton Assembly!

> *(***CHARLOTTE***-as-Lizzy starts galliarding.)*

TREVOR. Is Bongley –

JESSICA. Bingley.

TREVOR. Is he here? Does he like us?

JESSICA. He's here. And he brought a friend.

---

* A license to produce *The Complete Works of Jane Austen* does not include a performance license for any third-party or copyrighted recordings. Licensees should create their own.

TREVOR. Two bachelors!

JESSICA. Victory! Bingley likes Jane!

TREVOR. Sister Jane? Welsh pudding Jane?

JESSICA. That's the one.

TREVOR. How does Lizzy feel about that?

JESSICA. Let's go down to the field and find out.

> (**JESSICA** *as Jane, in hat, to* **CHARLOTTE** *as Lizzy.)*

Mr. Bingley is just what a young man ought to be! I never saw such happy manners!

CHARLOTTE. *(As Lizzy.)* He is also handsome, which a young man ought likewise to be, if he possibly can. Well, I give you leave to like him. You have liked many a stupider person.

> (**CHARLOTTE**-*as-Lizzy resumes galliarding.)*

TREVOR. So Lizzy's not into the Bings? What about his friend?

JESSICA. Introducing...

> *(Produces Darcy hat.)*

The leading man. Fitzwilliam Darcy. Brooding and often misunderstood. Margaret Atwood blames Jane Austen for dooming young readers "to a series of initially hopeful liaisons in which unpleasant men turn out to be simply unpleasant." She likes a dark horse, our girl Jane Austen.

> (**JESSICA** *puts on the Bingley hat; gives Darcy's hat to* **TREVOR**, *who just holds it.)*

(As Bingley.) Come Darcy, I must have you dance. I hate to see you standing about by yourself in this stupid way. You had much better dance.

TREVOR. *(As Darcy.)* Um. I don't feel like it.

JESSICA. Yeah, put it on.

(Puts Darcy's hat on **TREVOR**'s *head.)*

TREVOR. *(As Darcy, in full.)* You know how I detest dancing –

(Hat off, as **TREVOR**.*)*

Whoa. That's incredible. I've never read this book!

JESSICA. Harry, never underestimate the importance of the right hat.

(TREVOR *puts the hat back on.)*

TREVOR. *(As Darcy.)* You know how I detest dancing unless I am particularly acquainted with my partner. Your sisters are engaged, and there is not another woman in the room whom it would not be a punishment to stand up with. You are dancing with the only handsome girl in the room.

JESSICA. *(As Bingley.)* Miss Elizabeth Bennet is standing just behind you –

(CHARLOTTE-*as-Lizzy runs next to* **TREVOR** *with fan.)*

Who is very pretty and, I dare say, very agreeable.

TREVOR. *(As Darcy.)* She is...tolerable, but not handsome enough to tempt me.

(Quickly pulls hat off.)

Oh! Whoa! Bad hat! Very bad!

(To **JESSICA**.*)* But did Lizzy hear?

CHARLOTTE. *(As Lizzy.)* I could easily forgive *his* pride, if he had not mortified *mine*.

JESSICA. Time to re-draw battle plans.

> (**JESSICA** *unrolls a map;* **CHARLOTTE** *does her best "Mrs. Bennet as Army General" impression, with the hat.*)

CHARLOTTE. *(As Mrs. B.)* OKAY! Jane has received an invitation to visit Mr. Bingley's sister for dinner at Netherfield Park. BUT! Mr. Bingley will be away that evening. SO! Jane is going to ride side saddle the three miles between Longbourn and the Bingley encampment AS it is likely to rain and Jane will be soaked THUS obligating the Bingleys to invite her to stay the night.

> (**JESSICA** *triumphantly re-rolls the map.*)

TREVOR. That's...

CHARLOTTE. *(As Mrs. B.)* Transparent.

TREVOR. Manipulative.

JESSICA. And it totally works. What's worse, Jane comes down with a cold and has to spend several days with the Bingleys. Lizzy arrives to nurse her and finds she has to spend time with Darcy.

> (**CHARLOTTE**-*as-Lizzy and* **TREVOR**-*as-Darcy put on hats and strike battle poses.*)

CHARLOTTE. *(As Lizzy.)* Your defect is a propensity to hate everybody.

TREVOR. *(As Darcy.)* And yours is willfully to misunderstand them.

JESSICA. Jane and Lizzy return home.

Please meet –

> (**JESSICA** *produces hat.*)

Mr. Collins.

CHARLOTTE. OOH, let me!

(Grabs hat.)

TREVOR. A bachelor!

CHARLOTTE. And a total boob.

*(**CHARLOTTE** puts on Collins' hat and drones on.)*

(As Collins.) Mrs. Bennet, you have so fine a family of daughters! I have heard, of course, of their beauty, but, in this instance, fame has fallen short of truth. I do not doubt in your seeing them all, in due time, disposed of in marriage. I am very sensible, madam, of the hardship to my fair cousins...

*(This will be a while – **JESSICA** talks over Collins' droning.)*

JESSICA.	CHARLOTTE.
Okay, land entails. Where to start?	*(As Collins.)* I cannot be otherwise than concerned at being the means of injuring your amiable daughters, and beg leave to apologize for it, as well as to assure you of my readiness to make them every possible amends.
TREVOR.	
(Has pulled out his phone.) "A form of trust established by deed which restricts the inheritance of real estate property to an heir – usually male – by operation of law."	
(Looks over at Collins.) Oh no.	I could say much on the subject, but that I am cautious of appearing forward and precipitate.

JESSICA.	**CHARLOTTE.**
Yup. Longbourn belongs to that guy. And he's come for a visit. Wrap it up!	But I can assure the young ladies that I come prepared to admire them.

CHARLOTTE. *(As Collins.)* At present I will not say more.

JESSICA. Welcome to another Austen type – the bumbling clergyman.

CHARLOTTE. *(To* **JESSICA.***)* You have to speed it up! We haven't even gotten to Wickham yet.

JESSICA. He's next!

(Hat!)

Introducing: The Cad.

(Tosses it to **TREVOR,** *who puts it on.)*

TREVOR. *(As Wickham.)* It was the prospect of constant society and good society which was my chief inducement to enter the shire. *(Taking the hat off and looking at it.)* How does it do that?

JESSICA. And Lizzy is one smitten kitten.

Turns out that Wickham and Darcy grew up together but there was a falling out. And Darcy didn't secure Wickham a position in the clergy so he had to join the army.

CHARLOTTE & TREVOR. Gasp!

JESSICA. Next:

(Regency dance music plays.)*

Netherfield ball!

CHARLOTTE. Bingley and Jane seem to be falling in love!

---

* A license to produce *The Complete Works of Jane Austen, Abridged* does not include a performance license for any third-party or copyrighted recordings. Licensees should create their own.

(The crowd roars.)

JESSICA. But what's this?

CHARLOTTE. Wickham doesn't seem to be anywhere –

TREVOR. WHO WILL LIZZY DANCE WITH?!

CHARLOTTE. Cousin Collins.

(Disappointed groan from the crowd.)

JESSICA. And Darcy.

TREVOR. Darcy? But they hate each other.

JESSICA. Do they?

*(**CHARLOTTE** and **TREVOR** don Lizzy and Darcy hats.)*

CHARLOTTE. *(As Lizzy.)* I remember hearing you once say that you hardly ever forgave, that your resentment once created was unappeasable. You are very cautious, I suppose, as to its being created.

TREVOR. *(As Darcy.)* I am.

CHARLOTTE. *(As Lizzy.)* And you never allow yourself to be blinded by prejudice?

TREVOR. *(As Darcy.)* May I ask to what these questions tend?

CHARLOTTE. *(As Lizzy.)* Merely to the illustration of your character; I am trying to make it out.

TREVOR. *(As Darcy.)* And what is your success?

CHARLOTTE. *(As Lizzy.)* I do not get on at all.

JESSICA. Next! The rules of engagement: Lizzy's first proposal!

TREVOR. A proposal?! From whom...

(**CHARLOTTE** *clears throat as* **JESSICA** *puts Collins' hat on her.*)

Oh no.

CHARLOTTE. *(As Collins.)* Permit me to assure you in the most animated language of the violence of my affection –

(As Lizzy, changing hats.) Yeah. That's a hard no.

JESSICA. See! Right there! That's why it's not just about marriage. Collins is actually a good catch. He's a man with a position and a home. Lizzy's best friend Charlotte Lucas –

CHARLOTTE. Smart, wonderful Charlotte!

JESSICA. – actually ends up accepting a proposal from Collins just a few days later. But Lizzy says no. Austen is asking more of her readers.

CHARLOTTE. Next!

JESSICA. Bingley dumps Jane!

TREVOR. What?

CHARLOTTE. Stone cold.

JESSICA. It's a whole thing, but just take the plot point for now.

So! Jane goes off to visit family in London to heal her heartbreak. Lizzy passes some lonely months before she goes to visit Charlotte and Mr. Collins at Hunsford Parsonage. It turns out that Mr. Collins works for a super fancy rich lady –

(Hat!)

Lady Catherine de Bourgh. She makes Margaret Thatcher look like Mother Teresa. Turns out she's also Darcy's aunt.

CHARLOTTE. So, so much happens on this visit –

JESSICA. Lizzy learns from Fitzwilliam, Darcy's mouthy cousin –

CHARLOTTE. So, so mouthy.

JESSICA. – that it was Darcy who inveigled to keep Jane and Bingley apart.

TREVOR. No!

CHARLOTTE. And Lizzy and Darcy go to battle, right there in his aunt's house.

TREVOR. *(As Darcy, in hat.)* I am not afraid of you.

JESSICA. And then he proposes –

TREVOR. *(As Darcy.)* In vain I have struggled.

Your inferiority, a degradation.

Despite all endeavors, I have found it impossible to conquer my feelings.

My hope is that I will now be rewarded by your acceptance of my hand.

 (Takes hat off.)

Oh, yuck! *(To* **JESSICA** *and* **CHARLOTTE.***)*

She says no, doesn't she?

JESSICA & CHARLOTTE. Yup.

JESSICA. So, again, it's not / just about marriage.

TREVOR. Just about marriage. He didn't respect her.

CHARLOTTE. Exactly. So it doesn't matter how loaded he is.

TREVOR. What happens next?

JESSICA & CHARLOTTE. The letter!

CHARLOTTE. Darcy writes this letter!

JESSICA. It explains everything.

CHARLOTTE. Turns out Wickham had seduced Darcy's fifteen-year-old sister!

TREVOR. Ew!

JESSICA. In an effort to secure her fortune for himself!

TREVOR. No!

CHARLOTTE. Darcy saved the day and convinced his sister of Wickham's true intent!

TREVOR. Whew!

JESSICA. But his sister was heartbroken and it took her months to recover!

TREVOR. Aw!

CHARLOTTE. And then Darcy rationalizes the whole Jane thing –

TREVOR. Bings! Why?!

JESSICA. And then comes THE moment:

CHARLOTTE. *(As Lizzy, in hat.)* How despicably I have acted. I who have prided myself on my discernment. I who have valued myself on my abilities. How humiliating this discovery. Had I been in love I could not have been more wretchedly blind. But vanity, not love, has been my folly. Till this moment I never knew myself!

JESSICA. Self-actualized truth bomb.

TREVOR. Well...

JESSICA. Yes?

TREVOR. Can I just point out that every exchange he's had with her up to now has been...well, he's been really rude. Like...super rude. This hat has made me say some very rude things. Unless you guys skipped over some scene where he shows up with, like, tea and homemade muffins.

CHARLOTTE. No, we didn't.

TREVOR. So is Lizzy really prejudiced? Or was she just responding to the stimuli she was given?

(A beat.)

JESSICA. Oh my god, do you see how many Janeites are here? Are you trying to start a war?

TREVOR. Well, I just –

CHARLOTTE.   **JESSICA.**
Nope!   Not happening!

JESSICA. Anyway!

So you know how in every battle movie, there's the quiet before the storm where everyone just hunkers down and re-groups?

TREVOR. The night before the Battle of Helm's Deep.

JESSICA. Yeah. Sure. So that's where we are right now. Jane and Lizzy return to Longbourn. But, important exposition – the militia, including Wickham, is leaving town, and they're headed to Brighton. It's like the [Down the Shore] of England. Kitty and Lydia are distraught.

(Sobbing handfuls of ribbons fly through the air.)

Until Lydia is invited to go to Brighton with some family friends.

(One sobbing handful of ribbons and one ecstatically happy one.)

Kitty was the sad one.

TREVOR. Got it.

JESSICA. So off Lydia goes, despite serious objections from Lizzy.

CHARLOTTE. *(As Lizzy, in hat.)* Lydia is only sixteen.

She will be the most determined flirt that ever made herself and her family ridiculous.

JESSICA.   FAST FORWARD! Lizzy is invited to tour Derbyshire with her uncle and aunt. And you'll never guess who lives there...

TREVOR. Who?

CHARLOTTE. Fitzwilliam Darcy!

> **(CHARLOTTE** *puts on the hat, becomes Lizzy, and trots around the stage in a "carriage.")*

JESSICA. So, off Lizzy goes with uncle and aunt.

CHARLOTTE. *(As Lizzy.)* What are men to rocks and mountains?

> **(CHARLOTTE**-*as-Lizzy continues trotting.)*

TREVOR. There are mountains in England?

JESSICA. And pretty soon, after finding out Darcy is supposed to be away, they go see Pemberley, the Darcy family estate. And it's –

CHARLOTTE. *(As Lizzy. Seeing the house.)* Holy shit.

TREVOR. That's in Austen?

JESSICA. Basically.

CHARLOTTE. *(As Lizzy.)* And of this I might have been mistress!

JESSICA. And guess who's not away...

TREVOR. Darcy??

JESSICA. He's just come in from a hot afternoon of riding hard –

CHARLOTTE. Oh boy. Jessica.

JESSICA. And so he strips off his shirt –

CHARLOTTE. No, he doesn't.

JESSICA. And he's just the right balance of muscle-y and real, with the perfect soupçon of chest hair –

CHARLOTTE. *(Chastising.)* You know that's not in the book! That's not even in the BBC!

JESSICA. SHUT UP AND LET ME HAVE THIS.

> *(Resuming.)*

And dives, in just his breeches, into a perfect summer pond –

TREVOR. His house is so fancy it has a name but he's bathing in a pond?

JESSICA.	**CHARLOTTE.**
Shhhhh!	She will kill you.

JESSICA. And he emerges from the water with the perfect toss of his dark, wet hair.

> *(She collapses.)*

CHARLOTTE. Okay, yeah, she's going to be incapacitated for a while so I'll take it from here. Lizzy and Darcy bump into each other!

> *(They don their hats.)*

TREVOR. *(As Darcy.)* ...

CHARLOTTE. *(As Lizzy.)* ...

TREVOR. *(As Darcy.)* ...

CHARLOTTE. *(As Lizzy.)* ...

TREVOR. *(Removing the hat.)* I don't understand this. Whenever I put Darcy's hat on before, his words just popped out of my mouth.

CHARLOTTE. Oh yeah. That's because Austen didn't script this part.

TREVOR. What?

CHARLOTTE. It's full narration. She does that from time to time. But she does tell us –

(Becoming Lizzy.)

Why is he so altered? From what can it proceed? It cannot be for me – it cannot be for my sake that his manners are thus softened. It is impossible that he should still love me.

TREVOR. So the visit goes well?!

CHARLOTTE. Very well. The Bingleys arrive and the Bingster asks incessantly about Jane so Lizzy knows there's some hope there and then –

JESSICA. *(Suddenly revived.)* Another letter!

CHARLOTTE. There she is!

JESSICA. Word arrives that Lydia has run off with Wickham from Brighton. And you know they're probably doing the nasty.

CHARLOTTE. The whole family will be disgraced.

JESSICA. Back to Longbourn! Everyone is out of their mind with worry and then – poof! – word arrives that Wickham will marry Lydia. Scandal averted.

TREVOR. So he's not a bad guy?

JESSICA & CHARLOTTE. No, no. He's very bad.

CHARLOTTE. Lydia and Wickham return to Longbourn as husband and wife.

JESSICA. She's insufferable. But guess who's coming back to Netherfield?

TREVOR. The Bings!

CHARLOTTE. And Darcy is with him!

JESSICA. Finish him!

So basically, Bings flirts around a lot to see if Jane still digs.

She does.

He proposes.

It sounds like this.

> *(Puts both hats on at once.)*

...

...

...

TREVOR. Full narration again?

TREVOR, CHARLOTTE & JESSICA. Aw, come on!

JESSICA. Everyone's happy, but then –

> *(Thunder clap. The sounds of rain.* **JESSICA** *raises the Lady Catherine de Bourgh hat and puts it on* **TREVOR. CHARLOTTE** *dons the Lizzy hat.)*

And this one she wrote:

TREVOR. *(As Lady C.)* You can be at no loss, Miss Bennet, to understand the reason of my journey hither.

CHARLOTTE. *(As Lizzy.)* I have not been at all able to account for the honor of seeing you here.

TREVOR. *(As Lady C.)* I am not to be trifled with. However insincere you may choose to be, you shall not find me so. A report of a most alarming nature has reached me that Miss Elizabeth Bennet would, in all likelihood, be united to my own nephew, Mr. Darcy. Though I know it to be a scandalous falsehood.

CHARLOTTE. *(As Lizzy.)* If you believed it impossible to be true, I wonder that you took the trouble of coming so far.

(Battle stances.)

JESSICA. And so it went – blow for blow.

*(They fight. **TREVOR**-as-Lady C has the worst.)*

TREVOR. *(As Lady C.)* I take no leave of you, Miss Bennet. I send no compliments to your mother. You deserve no such attention. I am most seriously displeased.

*(**TREVOR** takes Lady C hat off, shudders.)*

Oh, she's scary.

JESSICA. Darcy returns. We find out it was Darcy who paid off Wickham and got him to marry Lydia. It becomes clear that he and Lizzy like each other. Like, *like* each other.

TREVOR. *(As Darcy, in hat.)* You are too generous to trifle with me. If your feelings are still what they were last April, tell me so at once. My affections and wishes are unchanged; but one word from you will silence me on this subject forever.

CHARLOTTE. *(As Lizzy.)* ...

TREVOR. *(Removing the hat.)* Full narration again?

JESSICA. Narration. But she does give us: "Elizabeth now forced herself to speak; and immediately, though not very fluently, gave him to understand that her sentiments had undergone so material a change, since the period to which he alluded, as to make her receive with gratitude and pleasure his present assurances."

CHARLOTTE. Paternal permission is sought and granted.

*(Becoming Lizzy again as **TREVOR** becomes Darcy.)*

How could you begin?

TREVOR. *(As Darcy.)* I cannot fix on the hour or the spot or the look or the words which laid the foundation. I was in the middle before I knew I had begun.

CHARLOTTE. *(As Lizzy.)* Now be sincere, did you admire me for my impertinence?

TREVOR. *(As Darcy.)* For the liveliness of your mind I did.

(**TREVOR** *takes off his hat.*)

Hey. Good job, hat.

(**JESSICA** *has started circling them.*)

JESSICA. Pppppkow! Coo! Coo! Sspppsh ssppshh!

CHARLOTTE. What are you doing?

JESSICA. Releasing doves and setting off fireworks. Pppppkow! Coo! Coo! Sspppsh ssppshh!

TREVOR. A game of survival. And Lizzy won.

JESSICA. Nah, bitch. Love did.

Scene Four

TREVOR. Okay, that hat really inspired me. So, I decided to try and read the books real quick. You know, for hat-context.

JESSICA. Naturally.

CHARLOTTE. Where'd you start?

TREVOR. I'm kind of reading all of them?

(Pulls out six opened books, stacked one upon another.)

Well, I'm only halfway through each one, but I think I've read enough to guess where they're all heading if we want to keep going.

CHARLOTTE. Yeah? Let's see. Lay some synopses on me.

JESSICA. Yeah, pop quiz! Give us some recaps.

TREVOR. OK? OK! OK. There's *Sense and Sensibility*, the story of two sisters staying exactly the same by marrying guys exactly like them: Edward and Willoughby.

CHARLOTTE. No. *Sense and Sensibility* is the story of how two sisters change, learning and growing as they come of age. And spoiler alert: Willoughby sucks.

TREVOR. Oh, huh. Would not have seen that coming. So then there's *Emma*: the story of an excellent matchmaker who sets her new friend Harriet up with Mr. Elton and never marries herself.

JESSICA. Oh honey. Emma finds that she is a terrible matchmaker. She marries her dear friend, and Harriet marries the man she loves who Emma originally wrote off as a bumpkin. OH. Have you seen *Clueless*? It's this.

CHARLOTTE. And Mr. Elton also sucks. Also spoiler alert.

TREVOR. ...OK. Maybe I need to keep reading. Lotta twists here.

JESSICA. Jane was the English countryside's M. Night Shyamalan.

CHARLOTTE. I see Regency people.

JESSICA. Oh, Charlotte. No.

TREVOR. OK but *Northanger Abbey* is definitely a horror story, right?

CHARLOTTE. *Northanger Abbey* is a parody of gothic novels. A young woman with an overactive imagination visits the titular –

(**JESSICA** *giggles throughout the following.*)

– the titular estate. She expects it to be gothic and scary and convinces herself that there was a murder on the premises, but it's actually all fine and dandy, at least murder-wise.

JESSICA. Titular!

TREVOR. OK, um. Next. *Mansfield Park* is the story of a moralizing young woman growing up with her rich and generally awful relations?

CHARLOTTE. Basically!

TREVOR. YES. And she...marries...her cousin Edmund who she loves and who doesn't suck?

CHARLOTTE. Bingo.

TREVOR. YES.

And then *Persuasion* –

CHARLOTTE. Is a gorgeous, mature love story about Anne Elliot and Frederick Wentworth who were engaged, then broken up, and then find their way back together eight years later. It's aching and redemptive and –

JESSICA. Chuck. Enough.

CHARLOTTE. Never.

> *(Tense staring moment between* **JESSICA** *and* **CHARLOTTE.***)*

Scene Five

CHARLOTTE. All right. Between the hat, the reading, and our...gentle corrections...do you think you're good to go?

TREVOR. Yeah! I think I got it.

But...well...OK. I admit I'm new to this and all, but guys? I think *Northanger Abbey* is my favorite. And that seems...unpopular with the both of you. But, for me, it's the one that's got the most...stuff in it.

JESSICA. Stuff?

TREVOR. Yeah. This girl Catherine goes on her vacation and all this STUFF happens, like cart rides with skeevy dudes, a possible ghost in the cupboard, a middle-of-the-night eviction. She meets this young clergyman who doesn't mind talking about novels and dresses – instant chemistry! But her sugar-daddy-seeking "friend" tries to keep them apart. Meanwhile, Clergyman's dad thinks Catherine's rich, so he brings her to Northanger only to find she is not rich so he turfs her out in the middle of the night. Catherine has to get home alone! Which is SCARY. But before all that, she says some dumb things about Clergyman's dead mom so maybe he never wants to see her again! But then he shows up at her house! And then they're in love. Ergo. Etc. Ba-da bing. Stuff!

JESSICA. But Harry, Austen's best books aren't about "stuff happening" – they are about the characters, finding –

CHARLOTTE. Catherine Morland is a silly bumpkin with silly notions in her head who falls in love with a pretty boring hero who was only made somewhat interesting by halfway implying his father murdered his own mother. Jane was only eighteen when she wrote it – it reads like a regency *Sweet Valley High* novel with shades of *Dungeons & Dragons*.

TREVOR. YES. I LOVE D&D. That's a great way to describe it!

JESSICA. I'm not sure we have to…

TREVOR. Challenge accepted.

> *(He rushes out of the room and returns with a D&D kit.)*

CHARLOTTE. What's. Happening?

TREVOR. *(Setting up as he talks.)* OK. This is perfect. It's like you keep saying, right? Jane is the storyteller in all her books! She's got a pretty distinct voice – so in a sense, she is the Dungeon Master. Except right now, I'll be the Dungeon Master since she's dead and all. OK?

CHARLOTTE. But what…?

JESSICA. Yeah. What do we…?

TREVOR. OK. I'll back it up. The DM is the god-like figure, the master storyteller. I make the world, you guys decide what happens, and then we see if you succeed or fail in your quests. OK. Just sit. Here's a pencil and paper each – it's got all sorts of stuff on there that will become important later…just try it out?

CHARLOTTE.	**JESSICA.**
Ummm…OK.	All right…

> *(They sit and begin playing.)*

TREVOR. Our story begins in the dark recesses of Northanger Abbey, the ancestral house of the Tilneys, a family of dubious origin and even worse communication skills. You have just concluded dinner – an awkward affair where the patriarch, General Tilney, a…

> *(Choosing a D&D designation.)*

wizard of questionable morals who may or may not be trying to bed the young heroine that he believes to have a large fortune...her name is...

(Turns to **JESSICA**.*)*

What's your character's name and what are you?

JESSICA. *(Reading her papers.)* Catherine the Poet, a Bard of the Clan of Morland. Wait – our heroine is a bard?

CHARLOTTE. Well, she does love a good story. Sounds right to me.

TREVOR. Catherine – you are an outsider here, young and uneducated in the ways of the world but willing to learn and full of many ideas. What you lack in poise, you make up for in gumption and needless dramatics. You are guided on your first journey through the darkened hallways of Northanger Abbey by...what are you?

CHARLOTTE. *(Reading.)* Henry Tilney, a Druid. I am gifted at reading novels, I know a lot about muslin, and I excel at being a lesser Jane Austen romantic lead.

TREVOR. You two must journey through the cold, unfeeling house fraught with money-grubbing sycophants, clueless brothers, and an odious and ill-tempered dragon to claim the – wait, what's the endgame here? What do Jane's heroines want?

JESSICA. Best question you've asked so far, Harry! It's certainly more than just being married. Right, Chuck?

CHARLOTTE. Yeah – Jane wrote about what she knew, and in Jane's time she knew a woman needed security and a home. But she's pretty realistic: like Jane says: "Nothing can be compared to the misery of being bound without Love." And she shows us plenty of couples in that predicament.

JESSICA. So for Jane's heroines, the goal is to find the right partner, rather than the convenient one, to give themselves the best shot at both security and happiness.

TREVOR. Not very D&D. I'm sticking with the dragon. We'll call him Rob.

JESSICA.	**CHARLOTTE**.
But –	Rob the dragon?

TREVOR. Catherine and Henry have entered the Abbey hall, which leads to Rob's lair. There is a sickening lurch as the dragon awakens…

> *(He looks expectantly at* **JESSICA** *and* **CHARLOTTE**, *like they know what they are doing.)*

Catherine, your initiative!

JESSICA. Wait. What? What do I – ? What happens now?

TREVOR. Just go with it – what would young Catherine do in this situation?

JESSICA. Um. Blush incessantly and agonize over it to her one and only friend? Make better choices next time? Practice avoidance? Journaling!

TREVOR. Think more D&D. Little more action, less angst.

JESSICA. Oh, OK. Ummm…young Catherine summons her rhyming rage to swing her quill, affectionately called "Ann Radcliffe," in the general direction of the dragon…?

> *(***TREVOR*** *rolls a die.)*

TREVOR. One. Critical failure. You miss Rob, which only causes him to get madder. Chuck?

CHARLOTTE. *(Somewhat getting into it now.)* Henry summons all his powers befitting his Wildfire 5e subclass to conjure an acid splash cantrip directly aimed at the fiendish creature...

JESSICA. You're a colossal nerd, Chuck.

CHARLOTTE. It's not without its appeal.

TREVOR. *(Rolls a die.)* Twenty! Critical hit. Henry has dealt a mortal blow to Rob –

> *(From* **CHARLOTTE***, a gesture of triumph – maybe a kick.)*

JESSICA. *(Not unkindly.)* I'm just not feeling this.

TREVOR. What's wrong?

JESSICA. We have our own nerd culture, thanks.

> *(Beat.)*

Movies, societies, fanfiction, costumed assemblies –

CHARLOTTE. People have tried finishing her unfinished works –

JESSICA. And speculating on her biography –

CHARLOTTE. Lovingly crafting satirical plays cramming all her works into a tight [eighty] minutes!

TREVOR. OK, but you can get D&D figurines.

CHARLOTTE. I have a Jane Austen action figure AND a Jane-shaped cookie cutter.

TREVOR. *(Somewhat deflated.)* Oh, we probably have that, too? I'm not much of a baker.

JESSICA. Don't feel bad. Jane fandom is actually the FIRST nerd culture. Janeites set in motion the kinds of practices that now define all modern fandom, especially online: a worldwide community with its own personality, codes, and in-jokes. People credit the Trekkies, but it's us. Minutiae, memes, a little cosplay... we're the OG.

CHARLOTTE. The ur-nerds.

TREVOR. Oh no way. Thanks, Janeites!

JESSICA. You got it, Sweet Cheeks.

TREVOR. Let's make a deal: we celebrate your nerd culture now, and you celebrate mine next weekend with a full Regency England D&D campaign. It'll just take, like, two to nine hours.

CHARLOTTE. Deal. So then, moving on...*Emma?*

JESSICA. OOH. I've got an idea!

Scene Six

(Innocuous game show intro music.)*

JESSICA. *(As Emma.)* I am Emma Woodhouse, and this is...

For Love or Money, a Regency courtship game where bachelors compete against each other and a woman of marriageable age competes against time and poverty. Since I am the richest and most charming person of my own acquaintance, I have little intention of ever marrying, myself. So I will serve, instead, as your host and matchmaker.

Let's meet our contestants. Bachelor Number One is our young vicar, Mr. Elton.

*(**CHARLOTTE** appears, dressed as Elton.)*

CHARLOTTE. *(As Elton. With a self-satisfied bow.)* Ahh, the lovely Miss Woodhouse. You're number one, in my book.

JESSICA. *(As Emma.)* He's not half as clever or interesting as he thinks himself but where there is a wish to please, one ought to overlook, and one must overlook a great deal, in this case.

CHARLOTTE. *(As Elton.)* Delicately expressed, as ever. *(Proudly.)* I have ambitions beyond my means.

(Tries to take her hand; she avoids it.)

JESSICA. *(As Emma. Without enthusiasm.)* Why thank you, Mr. Elton. *(Redirecting **CHARLOTTE**-as-Elton)*

---

* A license to produce *The Complete Works of Jane Austen, Abridged* does not include a performance license for any third-party or copyrighted recordings. Licensees should create their own.

Our second Bachelor is the stepson of my beloved governess, raised in another part of the country by a formidable aunt – the mysterious Frank Churchill…

(An empty spotlight.)

JESSICA. Frank Churchill…

*(A long beat. **JESSICA**-as-Emma giggles nervously.)*

Alas, he has not yet arrived. *(Glancing at her note cards for reference.)* His aunt cannot spare him, but I am sure that it is the only reason for his late arrival and not because he's a self-centered man-child who is secretly engaged to someone already.

And finally, Bachelor Number Three is this entirely unremarkable farmer, Robert Martin.

(She pulls out a corn husk.)

CHARLOTTE. *(As Elton.)* Lovely Miss Woodhouse, with the greatest respect for your wisdom…that is a corn husk.

JESSICA. *(As Emma.)* It's Robert Martin.

CHARLOTTE. *(As Elton.)* It's an inanimate object.

JESSICA. *(As Emma.)* Precisely.

CHARLOTTE. *(As Elton.)* Corn is a new world crop, right? Do we even have corn in the Regency?

JESSICA. *(As Emma.)* Dramaturg?

(A bell dings twice.)

Dramaturg says yes! *(A beat.)* Let's meet our bachelorette!

*(**JESSICA**-as-Emma is hyping Harriet as she crosses to the exit, clearly planning a quick change into the character.)*

My lovely friend, whom literary critic John Mullan called "the dumbest character in all of fiction," Harriet Smith!

CHARLOTTE. *(As Elton.)* Wait, a second – Harriet Smith?! I'm not here to woo Harriet Smith. I am here for you alone, Miss Woodhouse!

JESSICA. *(As Emma. Starting to remove her bonnet or something.)* Don't you worry, she's gonna look just like me –

CHARLOTTE. *(As Elton.)* Harriet Smith!? She's the natural daughter of nobody knows who. Besides which, she's poor! Everybody has their level, but for me, a gentleman, it would be a degradation!

JESSICA. *(As Emma.)* The light of Christ just shines right through you, doesn't it, vicar?

We'll be right back after a brief word from our sponsors!

> *(**TREVOR**-as-Knightley enters, during the above.)*

TREVOR. *(As Knightley.)* Harriet Smith has some first-rate qualities, actually.

JESSICA. *(As Emma.)* Ah, Mr. Knightley. The truest gentleman that exists. I am so happy to see you. I am always so happy to see you. I just don't know what that means yet.

CHARLOTTE. *(As Elton.)* I know when I'm not wanted.

> *(**CHARLOTTE**-as-Elton leaves in a huff.)*

JESSICA. *(As Emma.)* Wait! We have a game to play. Where is he going?

TREVOR. *(As Knightley.)* Likely he's off to play Who Wants to Marry a Millionaire. He will find himself a Mrs. Elton who is as obnoxious as she is rich. Dear Emma, you would have chosen better for him than he will for himself.

JESSICA. *(As Emma.)* Well, now I'm *two* bachelors short. I do wish Mr. Frank Churchill would arrive. After a brief flirtation in which I fancy myself in love with him

> *(A small growl of displeasure from* **TREVOR**-*as-Knightley, then* **JESSICA**-*as-Emma continues conspiratorially to the audience.)*

– my plan is to fix him up with Harriet. Oh, they'll be charming!

TREVOR. *(As Knightley.)* You do not need an array of bachelors for Harriet Smith, dear Emma. That sensible farmer, my friend Robert Martin, is desperately in love and means to marry her. He told me everything. I never hear better sense from anyone than Robert Martin.

JESSICA. *(As Emma.)* For a corn husk. Anyway, I've already arranged the game so she'll refuse him.

TREVOR. *(As Knightley.)* Love is not a game, Emma. How could you?

JESSICA. *(As Emma.)* It is always incomprehensible to a man that a woman should ever refuse an offer of marriage. A man always imagines a woman to be ready for anybody who asks her.

TREVOR. *(As Knightley.)* Nonsense! A man does not imagine any such thing.

JESSICA. *(As Emma.)* Harriet is not a clever girl, but she is pretty enough to choose among any gentleman she should wish.

TREVOR. *(As Knightley.)* Men of sense do not want silly wives. Upon my word, Emma, better be without sense than misapply it as you do.

JESSICA. *(As Emma.)* There is nothing more to say on the subject. Good day to you, Mr. Knightley. I must go in search of additional bachelors to play.

(**CHARLOTTE**-*as-Mrs. Weston enters.*)

Why Mrs. Weston, my beloved governess. I wasn't expecting to see you in this radically simplified retelling. I thought I'd summarized you in the exposition.

CHARLOTTE.   *(As Mrs. Weston.)* Dearest Emma, I've only come to suggest that Mr. Knightley himself is an eligible bachelor. Perhaps he will be inclined toward our next bachelorette, Highbury's most accomplished young woman, Jane Fairfax?

JESSICA. *(As Emma.)* NO! What I mean is, I have no wish for Mr. Knightley to play. I have absolutely no self-awareness as to why. If you'll both excuse me, I must go make my quick change – I mean, bring Harriet out here.

(**JESSICA**-*as-Emma exits.*)

TREVOR.   *(As Knightley.)* I fear Emma was spoiled by being the cleverest of her family.

CHARLOTTE.   *(As Mrs. Weston.)* No! With all Emma's little faults, she is an excellent creature: there is not a better daughter, or a kinder sister, or a truer friend. And can you imagine anything nearer perfect beauty than Emma altogether? She is loveliness itself, Mr. Knightley, is she not?

TREVOR. *(As Knightley.)* I think her all you describe. I love to look at her. *(Beat.)* But my deeper feelings on this matter will go entirely uninvestigated for the present.

CHARLOTTE. *(As Mrs. Weston.)* Won't she make a perfect match for my stepson, Frank Churchill?

(**TREVOR**-*as-Knightley emits another small growl. Beat.*)

Well, my work here is done.

> *(As she exits,* **CHARLOTTE***-as-Mrs. Weston greets an entering* **JESSICA***-as-Harriet.)*

Miss Smith.

JESSICA. *(As Harriet.)* Oh, hello.

> *(***TREVOR***-as-Knightley bows.)*

(As Harriet.) Is Mr. Elton here? I was told to like him – um, look for him.

TREVOR. *(As Knightley.)* Regrettably, he has chosen not to remain.

JESSICA. *(As Harriet. Feelingly.)* Oh! My heart is broken into little pieces. I loved him. *(Recovering.)* But you're here. And very elegant. And you're talking to me!

TREVOR. *(As Knightley.)* I am happy enough to keep you company, Miss Smith.

JESSICA. *(As Harriet.)* You are?! I will overestimate everything about this encounter!

TREVOR. *(As Knightley.)* Wouldn't you like to marry this nice corn husk?

JESSICA. *(As Harriet. Taking the corn husk enthusiastically.)* Yes! I would! *(Beat.)* Eventually.

> *(She begins to leave but is going the wrong way.* **TREVOR***-as-Knightley redirects her toward the exit, as appropriate for the production's set. In the original production, she tries first to go through the audience; this may be adjusted based on layout.)*

TREVOR. *(As Knightley.)* No, no, [that's the audience.]

> *(She tries again – still wrong. Perhaps she crosses up and knocks on the set wall.)*

[That's the wall.]

> (**JESSICA**-*as-Harriet looks up and points to the correct exit.*)

There you are. Very good.

> (**JESSICA**-*as-Harriet skips off.* **TREVOR**-*as-Knightley is alone.*)

(As Knightley.) This moment alone gives me time to contemplate my feelings. I am not enjoying the experience. I wonder if Emma has encountered Frank Churchill back there. They are intended for each other, after all, though surely he, a breezy conceited young man, cannot bring out the best in her. *(He emits a small growl, then, discovering:)* I am jealous of Frank Churchill. Which means I must be in love with Emma myself! And I always have been! Dearest Emma! Well, that's... *(Deflating.)* poor timing on my part. I will cross over there, to learn to be indifferent.

> *(He does so.* **JESSICA**-*as-Emma enters.)*

JESSICA. *(As Emma.)* Harriet has just told me that she believes Mr. Knightley to be in love with her! And Mr. Knightley is the last man in the world who would intentionally give any woman the idea of his feeling for her more than he really does. What a terrible mistake! But why should I be made so unhappy by the prospect of a union between my two friends? I must be in love with Mr. Knightley myself! And I always have been! My Mr. Knightley! Well, that's...poor timing on my part.

> *(She sees him.)*

Mr. Knightley!

TREVOR. *(As Knightley.)* Emma!

JESSICA. *(As Emma.)* Hello.

TREVOR. *(As Knightley.)* Hello.

JESSICA. *(As Emma.)* Hello. I already said that, didn't I? *(An attempt to recover.)* Have you heard? The unseen Frank Churchill has secretly been engaged to the unseen Jane Fairfax this whole time! No one saw that coming!

TREVOR. *(As Knightley.)* Time, my dearest, Emma, will heal the wound.

JESSICA. *(As Emma.)* You are kind, but you are mistaken. I have never been at all attached to him.

TREVOR. *(As Knightley.)* Emma, is this true? Then he is a fortunate man indeed.

JESSICA. *(As Emma.)* You speak as if you envied him.

TREVOR. *(As Knightley.)* I do envy him.

JESSICA. *(As Emma.)* Don't tell me why! Wait! Definitely tell me why! Just – as a friend. Super casual and friend-like.

TREVOR. *(As Knightley.)* As a friend! Emma, that I fear is a word – *(Stopping.)* Tell me, then, have I no chance of ever succeeding? My dearest Emma, for dearest you will always be, my dearest, most beloved Emma.

(**JESSICA**-*as-Emma is silent.*)

(As Knightley.) ...so that's a no?

JESSICA. *(As Emma.)* Oh, it's absolutely a yes! Jane Austen just didn't write my dialogue for this part. But she did write this: "She was his own Emma, by hand and word." And so I am your Emma.

*(Beat. **JESSICA** becomes herself again.)*

Good job!

TREVOR. *(Also himself again.)* You too! Such pathos!

JESSICA. Ohmigod thank you so much!

CHARLOTTE. *(Entering, holding spectacles, ready for her next role.)* Wait, what are you doing?

JESSICA. We finished *Emma.*

CHARLOTTE. Wait, that's it? What about the episode where they insult Miss Bates on Box Hill? I borrowed spectacles –

JESSICA. No thank you.

CHARLOTTE. But. No Knightley scolding Emma for calling Miss Bates ridiculous? *(Trying to put on the glasses quickly.)* We could just do it real quick –

JESSICA. It's one of the most painful scenes.

TREVOR. So we skipped to the hand-holding.

CHARLOTTE. Alright, I can read the room.

(Sad music plays.*)

---

* A license to produce *The Complete Works of Jane Austen, Abridged* does not include a performance license for any third-party or copyrighted recordings. Licensees should create their own.

Scene Seven

JESSICA. Right then. Moving on. Radical idea: let's skip *Mansfield Park.*

TREVOR. I would agree.

CHARLOTTE. Uh, no.

JESSICA. No one likes that one.

CHARLOTTE. Well, I do.

JESSICA. Yeah, well, most people do not.

TREVOR. It's consistently at the bottom of Austen's "Best Of" lists.

CHARLOTTE. How do you know that?

TREVOR. I asked Alexa.

CHARLOTTE. Of course.

JESSICA. So, we can say we said it and move on, yeah?

CHARLOTTE. No! No, we can't!

JESSICA. But why? It's so...I dunno...meh.

TREVOR. I concur. Meh.

CHARLOTTE. Why meh?

JESSICA. Unclear. Maybe the whole first cousins marrying each other thing?

TREVOR. Makes me squeamish. Have to admit.

CHARLOTTE. But, it's a tale of good overcoming crappiness. The good people win. The bad people get banished. Literally sent away to live with their horrible aunt – spoiler alert – for being cheaters.

JESSICA. Look. Fanny Price is boring, okay? She's dull and milquetoast-y...and dull.

CHARLOTTE. But she's steadfast and quiet and true and loves her brother a lot.

TREVOR. And one very particular cousin.

CHARLOTTE. Oh c'mon. Everyone did that. And Edmund's a good guy.

JESSICA. Guy who wants to be a preacher but falls in love with a pretty face who only wants a rich husband?

CHARLOTTE. Miss Crawford is captivating!

TREVOR. And a looker.

CHARLOTTE.	**JESSICA.**
Not helping.	Welsh pudding!

CHARLOTTE. It's like a Cinderella story. The bad sisters lose in the end. The sad yet virtuous Fanny wins out in the end.

JESSICA. She's dull. And she marries her first cousin. Doesn't play well with modern audiences.

TREVOR. I concur.

CHARLOTTE. I'll tell you who it will play well with. A really powerful, if odd, bunch of people. With disposable income. Because you remember who else is in that book, right? Don't you?

(**JESSICA** *and* **TREVOR** *look at* **CHARLOTTE** *blankly.)*

Right. I'll show you then. Nothing like a visual aid.

(**CHARLOTTE** *leaves the room. Returns with a pug. Could be stuffed. Could be real.)*

That's why. Lady Bertram's pug. Simply called Pug. We fire up those pug people and that book shoots to the top of the list.

(*Everyone stares at the pug.)*

JESSICA. But no one wants to shoot it up the list. I just don't think...

TREVOR. I concur.

CHARLOTTE. Believe me, they are weirdly powerful.

JESSICA. Heard and noted. And it seems to me you've just done it, then. Talked about the book, I mean. Well done. You got your weird pug plug in. Good for you. Can we move on?

> *(Beat –* **CHARLOTTE** *doesn't move.)*

Is it more than just pugs?

> *(***CHARLOTTE*** *mumbles something unintelligible – you know, Charlotte sounds.)*

JESSICA. I'm sorry, Chuck. I don't speak Mumble. Use your words. Jane is all about words.

TREVOR. I concur.

CHARLOTTE. The introverts.

JESSICA. What?

CHARLOTTE. It's for the introverts. The Fanny Prices of the world. The bravely quiet and terrified among us. That's why I love this book. They deserve some overdue attention. *(Beat.)* Right?

JESSICA. Absolutely.

CHARLOTTE. They deserve...wait. What? Thought you were going to fight me more on that one.

JESSICA. Not at all. I see your point. I am "yes, and"–ing this all day.

CHARLOTTE. Um. OK, then! Terrific! Then let's give it up for the Fannies of the world! Good people!

> *(Addressing the audience.)*

If you're a Fanny Price – a reserved, quiet soul who is kind, generous and loyal but will absolutely stand up for what's right and just – this is for you! Just hold up your hand or wave or merely blush and look flustered so you can be recognized!

> *(Hopefully, the shy people in the audience do this. Then* **TREVOR**, **CHARLOTTE**, *and* **JESSICA** *can give a really kind and reserved sort of applause for them. If not, actors can note that "Well, Fannies wouldn't really self-identify, would they?" and applaud the secret Fannies in the room.)*

JESSICA. You know, I'm glad we did that. Hooray for introverts!

Scene Eight

(A private conversation, to start.)

TREVOR. We have to do it.

CHARLOTTE. Why? Who's got the time?

JESSICA. We made time for *Mansfield*, Chuck.

TREVOR. They'll expect it, won't they?

CHARLOTTE. The Janeites will, but the newbies won't!

TREVOR. Come on. It'll be quick!

JESSICA. Like ripping off a bandaid!

TREVOR. These are so short! I finished them before I got halfway through the others.

JESSICA. It does say "the *complete* works" on the [postcard], not "the complete works minus everything that isn't one of the big six novels."

> *(Beat.)*

CHARLOTTE. Fair enough.

TREVOR. YES.

> *(To audience, in his glory.)* Thanks for your patience, folks! And now we present: The Lesser-Known Works!

> *(Movie trailer voice.)* In a world where gender roles are firm and girls have little agency, one child writer crafted wild stories, plays, and poems of female sensuality –

> **(CHARLOTTE** *demonstrates.)*

Lady drunkenness –

> **(JESSICA** *demonstrates.)*

And women doing violence and having adventures.

> (**CHARLOTTE** *air slaps* **JESSICA**, *who then air slaps* **CHARLOTTE**. *Both then turn and strike a fists-up pose at an unseen foe.*)

Jane Austen, aged eleven through seventeen, Presents: The Juvenilia. Rated, surprisingly, PG-13!

JESSICA. My turn!

(Movie trailer voice.) In a world where going to the beach is a cure for what ails you –

> (**TREVOR** *and* **CHARLOTTE** *relax, breathe the sea air deep.*)

One sleepy resort town will get more than it bargained for.

TREVOR. *(As Mr. Parker, entrepreneur.)* Come on down to Sanditon, seaside resort of tomorrow! Reserve your very own bathing machine!

JESSICA. But when –

(Regular voice.) Oh shoot. Actually, Jane didn't finish this one.

(Back to movie trailer.) SANDITON: It's no day at the beach.

CHARLOTTE. OK fine, I'll take one.

(Movie trailer voice.) In a world where one daughter raised by a wealthy aunt will give her poorer sisters the education of a lifetime, things...will...happen.

THE WATSONS: Jane only wrote five chapters of this one!

(Regular voice, to **TREVOR**.*)* Bring it home, kid!

TREVOR. IN A WORLD...

Where novels are written entirely in correspondence, the pen is mightier than the sword.

Meet Lady Susan:

JESSICA. *(As Susan.)* Dear Mrs. Johnson,

I am so frighteningly beautiful, witty, and smart. I also seduce married men; scheme to marry off my unwilling daughter; and am otherwise dreadful. You know you love me.

Affectionately yours,

TREVOR. *(Movie trailer voice.)* LADY SUSAN: Jane definitely finished this one.

CHARLOTTE. Now I want popcorn. Was there popcorn in the Regency? Dramaturg?

> *("No" bell.)*

JESSICA. So they had corn, but didn't know how to pop it.

TREVOR. Bummer.

CHARLOTTE. And now I'm hungry.

JESSICA. Well, good thing we're so close!

TREVOR. What's next?

CHARLOTTE. *Sense and Sensibility*!

TREVOR. How do we do it?

JESSICA. Two women and one dude playing two sisters, three suitors, two antagonists, a lousy brother, a dear departed father, and narrators.

TREVOR. Easy!

> *(Three-way high-five.)*

Scene Nine

(A note on this scene: Though still listed as **TREVOR, JESSICA,** *and* **CHARLOTTE,** *they should narrate in plummy British dialects. Think Masterpiece Theatre.)*

TREVOR. *(Narrating.)* The sisters Dashwood, Elinor

*(***CHARLOTTE*** waves as Elinor.)*

and Marianne

*(***JESSICA*** waves as Marianne.)*

were exceedingly handsome, but not exceedingly wealthy. When their father passed away, his son inherited the estate, and most of the money, thanks to entail rules that pass things through the male line.

EVERYONE. Patriarchy!

TREVOR. *(As Father.)* Promise me you'll take care of your sisters and stepmother, son.

CHARLOTTE. *(As John.)* Uh, well –

TREVOR. *(As Father.)* PROMISE ME.

CHARLOTTE. *(As John.)* Okay!

*(***TREVOR***-as-Father smiles and dies.)*

(As John. To **JESSICA,** *who is playing Fanny.)* My dearest Fanny, for you are now playing my wife and that is your name, I promised my father I'd look after the girls, for they've no fortune of their own. What say you to giving them three thousand pounds apiece?

JESSICA. *(As Fanny.)* Yes that sounds fair, but what if…less?

CHARLOTTE. *(As John.)* Your argument is sound. One thousand?

JESSICA. *(As Fanny.)* You are so generous, my love. Certainly that will do for them, even if it means our own dear little boy will starve.

CHARLOTTE. *(As John.)* *(As if bargaining.)* How right you are. Five hundred?

JESSICA. *(As Fanny.)* *(As if bargaining too.)* Four.

CHARLOTTE. *(As John.)* Three.

JESSICA. *(As Fanny.)* One-fifty.

CHARLOTTE. *(As John.)* A HEARTY HANDSHAKE AND SOME GOOD WISHES.

JESSICA. *(As Fanny.)* That seems more than your father could reasonably expect. Sold.

(Narrating.) While Marianne and their mother could scarcely wait to be gone from the house, there was one thing making Elinor wish to stay: she was in love with Fanny's brother, Edward Ferrars.

> *(**TREVOR** cuts a dashing figure, and tips his cap, readying to play Edward.)*

(Narrating.) Hold your horses. Here's how Jane Austen describes him.

> *(Grabs a book.)*

"He was not handsome, and his manners required intimacy to make them pleasing."

TREVOR. *(Narrating.)* Fine.

> *(Begrudgingly takes on a painfully shy, shrunken posture – more worm than man.)*

CHARLOTTE. *(Narrating.)* "BUT when his natural shyness was overcome, his behavior gave every indication of an open, affectionate heart."

> *(**TREVOR**-as-Edward smiles. A little.)*

JESSICA. *(Narrating.)* Elinor was certain of Edward's feelings, but as he was terribly shy and she was prudent and reserved, neither had spoken of it.

> **(CHARLOTTE**-*as-Elinor and* **TREVOR**-*as-Edward both breathe in as if to speak, then look away.)*

TREVOR. *(Narrating.)* And so the sisters Dashwood, Elinor

> **(CHARLOTTE**-*as-Elinor waves again.)*

and Marianne

> **(JESSICA**-*as-Marianne waves again.)*

prepared to set off with their mother –

JESSICA. *(As Marianne. A la* Hamilton.*)* And Peggy!

TREVOR. *(Narrating.)* – and Margaret, a third sister who shan't appear in this play because we haven't the people and she's less important. As I say, they readied to leave Sussex behind for Devonshire and Barton Cottage, a small house offered them at a reasonable rent from a distant relation.

CHARLOTTE. *(As Elinor. To* **TREVOR**-*as-Edward, with as much feeling as she can muster.)* Goodbye, Edward, and thank you for the many happy memories. We shall miss...the house.

TREVOR. *(As Edward. With as much feeling as he's capable of displaying.)* Bye.

> *(He backs away, shyly.)*

JESSICA. *(As Marianne. Full of Marianne-ness.)* Never again shall I encounter such pleasing carpet, or a more dear clock, or drapes with such deep feeling, or chairs with such wit, or a happier home as long as I live, never never never –

CHARLOTTE. *(As Elinor.)* We have about seven more minutes to tell the story.

JESSICA. *(As Marianne.) (Bursts into tears and runs out.)* You're so unfeeling, Elinor!

> **(CHARLOTTE**-*as-Elinor is amused and exits behind her. All three immediately reenter with suitcases.)*

TREVOR. *(Narrating.)* As a house, Barton Cottage, though small, was comfortable and compact –

JESSICA. *(Narrating, but with full Marianne emotion.)* But as a cottage it was defective, for the window shutters were not painted green, nor were the walls covered with honeysuckles.

CHARLOTTE. *(Narrating.)* But the women immediately set about making it a home, hanging Elinor's drawings on the walls and setting up Marianne's pianoforte.

One day, Marianne went for a walk, as the sisters were often pleased to do. But when a rainstorm burst overhead, disaster struck!

> **(JESSICA**-*as-Marianne falls, her ankle twisted.)*

JESSICA. *(As Marianne.)* Whatever shall I do?

CHARLOTTE. *(Narrating.)* Suddenly, out of the rain and fog, a man appeared.

> **(TREVOR** *sighs, cuts his shy Edward pose.)*

(Narrating.) No, this one's dashing.

TREVOR. *(Narrating.)* Oh, yay!

> *(Cuts a more dashing figure. He helps* **JESSICA**-*as-Marianne up.)*

(As Willoughby.) Ladies, forgive my impropriety.

> *(He helps* **JESSICA**-*as-Marianne sit down.*
> *She is already in love.)*

I must call on you again tomorrow, to see how you're faring. My name *(With a roguish wink.)* is Willoughby.

CHARLOTTE & JESSICA. *(Both narrating.)* Uh-oh.

CHARLOTTE. *(Narrating.)* Marianne and Willoughby became fast friends and constant companions, until the talk of the village was their certain engagement.

> *(As* **CHARLOTTE** *speaks, they do the things she mentions.)*

They danced, they went for long walks and carriage rides, they played music, and they laughed constantly, at everything and nothing. Until one day –

> *(***JESSICA***-as-Marianne bursts into tears and runs away.)*

TREVOR. *(As Willoughby.)* I must go.

CHARLOTTE. *(As Elinor.)* But why?

TREVOR. *(As Willoughby.)* Because.

CHARLOTTE. *(As Elinor.)* Ah, well then you must.

TREVOR. *(Narrating.)* So Willoughby left, and Marianne –

> *(***JESSICA***-as-Marianne enters weeping, crosses slowly to the other side, and bursts into fresh tears every time she sees something Willoughby touched before exiting on the other side.)*

JESSICA. *(As Marianne.)* He sang with me at that pianoforte. And that – THAT – was his chair. And one time that candle went out, and he...and he... *(Sobs.)*

CHARLOTTE. *(As Elinor.)* I too am missing someone, but I am extremely calm about it.

> (**TREVOR** *takes the Edward pose. She screams.*)

EDWARD! I mean – good day Edward how lovely it is to see you yes hi.

TREVOR. *(As Edward. Full of Edward-level feelings.)* Hello Elinor. I'd like to visit for a week.

CHARLOTTE. *(As Elinor.)* You didn't tell us you were coming!

TREVOR. *(As Edward.)* No one in these books ever does.

JESSICA. *(Narrating.)* Edward passed a lovely week with the Dashwoods, but seemed melancholy, without explanation.

> (**TREVOR**-*as-Edward calibrates the usual Edward pose to a slightly sadder one.*)

That is, until –

TREVOR. *(As Edward.)* I must go.

CHARLOTTE. *(As Elinor.)* But why?

TREVOR. *(As Edward.)* Because.

CHARLOTTE. *(As Elinor.)* Ah, well then you must.

JESSICA. *(Narrating.)* And so the days passed. Marianne sulked, and Elinor brooded – politely and amiably – wondering why Edward's feelings for her now seemed in doubt. *(To* **CHARLOTTE**-*as-Elinor.)* You could just ask him, you know.

> (**CHARLOTTE**-*as-Elinor gasps.*)

TREVOR. *(Narrating.)* As was periodically the case, the Dashwoods' host family had guests: the sisters Steele. Lucy Steele was handsome, but lurking underneath her unobjectionable manners was something sinister.

JESSICA. *(As Lucy.)* Oh Elinor, I've heard so much about you! I must say, I think you are my newest and best friend. I hear you love someone by the name of Ferrars; how charming that is! It's such a CRAZY COINCIDENCE that I am secretly engaged to Edward Ferrars! Whatever are the odds of such a thing? And how wonderful that it definitely won't break your heart at all that I'm going to marry him SO HARD while you pine away!

>   (**CHARLOTTE**-*as-Elinor registers this, in her Elinor-y way.* **TREVOR** *bursts in, book in hand.*)

TREVOR.   *(Narrating.)* WAIT. We forgot to introduce Brandon.

CHARLOTTE.   *(Narrating.)* OH, / whoops.

JESSICA.   *(Narrating.)* Must we?

>   (**TREVOR** *adopts a Brandon pose.*)

CHARLOTTE.   *(As Elinor.)* Colonel Brandon, Marianne. Marianne, Col. Brandon.

JESSICA.   *(As Marianne. Indifferently.)* Hi.

TREVOR.   *(As Brandon. In love immediately, and in his best, most dramatic Alan Rickman voice throughout.)* Hello, Miss Dashwood.

CHARLOTTE.   *(Narrating.)* Brandon was a good, solid –

JESSICA.   *(Narrating.) (Coughing.)* Boring –

CHARLOTTE.   *(Narrating.)* – loyal friend of the family.

JESSICA.   *(Narrating.)* Let's carry on shall we? It's London time!

CHARLOTTE.   *(Narrating.)* The sisters traveled to London for the season with most of the other important characters.

JESSICA.   *(Narrating.)* And Peggy?

TREVOR. *(Narrating.)* Not Peggy.

CHARLOTTE. *(Narrating.)* But Willoughby was there – and so was Brandon.

TREVOR. *(As Brandon.)* Elinor, I'm hearing things about your sister and Willoughby. Are they engaged?

CHARLOTTE. *(As Elinor.)* It's complicated.

TREVOR. *(As Brandon. Ominously and extremely Rickman-esque.)* Hmm. That is troubling.

JESSICA. *(As Marianne.)* Have you seen Willoughby?

> *(**TREVOR** looks around for him. **CHARLOTTE**-as-Elinor and **JESSICA**-as-Marianne stare at him.)*

TREVOR. *(Narrating.)* OH!

> *(Adopts his Willoughby pose.)*

JESSICA. *(As Marianne.)* Willoughby! It's so good to see you!

TREVOR. *(As Willoughby. Coldly.)* New town, who this?

> *(He leaves. **JESSICA**-as-Marianne bursts into tears.)*

CHARLOTTE. *(As Elinor.)* There there, Marianne, I'm sure there's an explanation.

JESSICA. *(As Marianne.)* Yes! He loves me and was just overcome! Or owing to the financial sensitivities on both our parts wishes to keep our love a secret from his family until we can amass some fortune! Or –

> *(**TREVOR** throws her a paper airplane letter, which **JESSICA**-as-Marianne retrieves.)*

> *(To audience member nearest the airplane.)* It's from my boyfriend!

> *(She reads it.)*

Dear Marianne,

I'm just not that into you.

Peace,

Willoughby

> *(She collects herself. Bursts into scream sobs.* **TREVOR**-*as-Brandon joins* **CHARLOTTE**-*as-Elinor.)*

TREVOR. *(As Brandon.)* Now that your sister sees the kind of man Willoughby is, I'll tell you my story: I have a ward, Beth. Willoughby seduced her and then left her, though she was pregnant.

CHARLOTTE. *(As Elinor.)* NO.

TREVOR. *(As Brandon.)* I KNOW. He went to London in search of a rich wife; his aunt found out about his indiscretion and disinherited him.

> *(***CHARLOTTE**-*as-Elinor goes to* **JESSICA**-*as-Marianne and comforts her. She gathers her up and they exit.)*

(Narrating.) The sisters left London and got some unfortunate news on the way: Edward's mother discovered his secret engagement to Lucy and disinherited him, settling his whole fortune on his brother, Robert.

(Oprah voice.) YOU get disinherited, and YOU get disinherited, and EVERYBODY –

> *(***CHARLOTTE**-*as-Elinor politely coughs, motions that they should continue; exits.)*

(Narrating.) More troubling still: Marianne had not recovered from her disappointment in London, and had taken to walking long hours, alone, in the rain –

JESSICA. *(As Marianne.)* As one does.

TREVOR. *(Narrating.)* Until one day –

(**JESSICA**-*as-Marianne coughs violently.*)

CHARLOTTE. *(As Elinor.)* She has a fever!

(**JESSICA**-*as-Marianne is settled; she is feverish and near death.* **CHARLOTTE**-*as-Elinor tends to her, patting her forehead, holding her hand.* **TREVOR**-*as-Willoughby approaches.*)

TREVOR. *(As Willoughby.)* I – Willoughby, just to be clear – must see her!

CHARLOTTE. *(As Elinor.)* No.

TREVOR. *(As Willoughby.)* That's a good point! Please tell her I married for money rather than love, and I shall never be happy.

CHARLOTTE. *(As Elinor.)* If she survives this broken-heart-slash-head-cold, I'll pass it along.

(*He exits.* **CHARLOTTE**-*as-Elinor continues nursing* **JESSICA**-*as-Marianne, when* **TREVOR**-*as-Brandon appears.*)

TREVOR. *(As Brandon.)* What can I do?

CHARLOTTE. *(As Elinor.)* Brandon. After all this time?

TREVOR. *(As Brandon. Wildly, wholeheartedly Rickman-y.)* Always.

JESSICA. *(Narrating. As she pops suddenly out of bed.)* When Marianne recovered –

(*A rapid exchange.*)

CHARLOTTE. *(As Elinor.)* You're better?!

JESSICA. *(As Marianne.)* Yup!

CHARLOTTE *(As Elinor.)*	**TREVOR** *(As Brandon.)*
Hooray!	Hooray!

JESSICA. *(Narrating.)* – the sisters returned to Barton Cottage, where yet more news was waiting: Lucy Steele has married Mr. Ferrars.

> *(**CHARLOTTE**-as-Elinor is wounded by this. **TREVOR**-as-Edward enters, and she is surprised.)*

CHARLOTTE. *(As Elinor.)* I imagine I must congratulate you, my dear friend.

TREVOR. *(As Edward.)* Not just yet, no. Lucy is now married to my brother, Robert. The fortune was all she truly wanted.

CHARLOTTE. *(As Elinor.)* So you're not –?

TREVOR. *(As Edward.)* I am not.

CHARLOTTE. *(As Elinor.)* So could we –?

TREVOR. *(As Edward.)* I'm here only to ask if you would.

> *(**CHARLOTTE**-as-Elinor jumps on him, then immediately remembers the audience, backs up, and they chastely shake hands. **JESSICA**-as-Marianne enters, clears her throat, and **TREVOR** switches to Brandon.)*

JESSICA. *(As Marianne.)* So, everyone thinks we should get married.

TREVOR. *(As Brandon.)* They do. As do I.

JESSICA. *(As Marianne.)* ...OK!

> *(She jumps on him, caring not at all about the audience. The actors line up, with **TREVOR** in the middle.)*

CHARLOTTE. *(Narrating.)* And so, both sisters were married.

(**TREVOR** *acts affectionately first as Edward, then Brandon, toward the two sisters respectively.*)

JESSICA. *(Narrating.)* Among the merits and the happiness of Elinor and Marianne, let it not be ranked as the least considerable, that though sisters –

TREVOR. *(Narrating.)* And living almost within sight of each other –

CHARLOTTE. *(Narrating.)* They could live without disagreement between themselves, or producing coolness between their husbands.

(**CHARLOTTE**-*as-Elinor and* **JESSICA**-*as-Marianne clasp hands in front of* **TREVOR**, *who shakes his own hand.*)

(*Everyone becomes themselves again.*)

JESSICA. We did it!

(**JESSICA** *and* **TREVOR** *high-five, and leave.* **CHARLOTTE** *remains.*)

CHARLOTTE. Wait! There's one more!

Scene Ten

CHARLOTTE. Right. Hi. Gosh. We haven't been left alone yet, have we? Hi. I'm, as you know by now, Charlotte. Or Chuck. Great. Got that covered. And I just know that any minute now Jessica and Harry will be right back to help me with this last one. *Persuasion*. Which, if you've been paying attention and I know you have, is my favorite. It wasn't always that way. I loved the books in, I think, the order they were written – *Northanger*, then *Sense and Sensibility, Pride and Prejudice*, then *Mansfield, Emma*, and so on. But *Persuasion* was the book I encountered last. So, if all the books were a flight of wines, this would be the port. You get my drift.

(Pause – still a bit awkward.)

Annnnny minute now. They'll be back.

(Whistles, hums, kills time – still awkward.)

OK. A little plot synopsis, good suggestion.

Well, our heroine is Anne Elliot, the middle daughter of a baronet who has fallen on hard times, mainly due to his terrible spending habits. Eight years prior, Anne received a proposal from an earnest young man of no title or fortune, Frederick Wentworth. She was, despite their mutual affection, *persuaded* to turn him down. And so, at the age of twenty-seven, Anne finds herself with no prospects and a family near financial ruin. The family decides to rent out the ancestral home to recoup debts and move to Bath. The home is rented to an admiral and his wife, who is the sister of, you guessed it, Frederick Wentworth, now a wealthy naval captain. Anne and Wentworth find themselves once again in each other's orbits, navigating the choppy waters – see what I did there? – of past hurts and revived emotions. And through a series of social encounters in which Anne proves herself to be level-headed and steadfast and a few chance conversations in which Wentworth discovers Anne never recovered from her rejection of him, they eventually, and achingly, reunite. It's... gorgeous.

So, yeah! That is why I love this book. But it also fits into how I want to see the world. You grow up, you have these lofty ideas of happiness and perfection and then life kinda slaps you around a bit and you readjust. You lower your expectations, you don't reach for the stars. And then, just when you're ready to accept ALL that, you encounter true happiness again. The awakening of hope. Jane completed this book only six months before she died. It speaks of a woman looking at life from the other side of parties, flirtations and romances to true love and true acceptance. Anne and Wentworth were always meant to be together but it needed to happen at the right time. They had to be ready to accept each other for who they truly were and who they truly loved. Like how I love *Persuasion* and Jessica loves *Pride and Prejudice*. We just have to be ready to accept the other...

Scene Eleven

(**JESSICA** *has snuck in for the end of the monologue.*)

JESSICA. Oh, Chuck, / that's –

CHARLOTTE. Jessica, I want to say something.

JESSICA. Me too. You first.

CHARLOTTE. No, you.

JESSICA. No, please.

CHARLOTTE. Be my guest.

CHARLOTTE.	**JESSICA.**
I do love *P&P*.	I borrowed some of your deodorant.

CHARLOTTE. You beautiful weirdo. That's what you had to tell me?

JESSICA. Aw, she called me beautiful.

(**CHARLOTTE** *makes Charlotte sounds.*)

No. Chuck, you got me there. I see why you're so into *Persuasion*.

CHARLOTTE. And I absolutely get your *P&P* situation.

(**TREVOR** *enters at the last second for "P&P situation."*)

TREVOR. You arguing about the books again? Dammit! *(Yells offstage.)* I owe you five bucks, Dramaturg!

(Dramaturg bell from Emma *dings.)*

CHARLOTTE & JESSICA. No, we're not!

TREVOR. YES. *(Yells offstage.)* YOU owe ME five bucks, Dramaturg!

(Sad version of dramaturg bell from Emma *dings.)*

CHARLOTTE. For the sake of Harry's fiver: You must allow me to tell you how ardently I admire and love you.

JESSICA. Well, Chuck, of course you do.

And I have no notion of loving people by halves. It is not my nature.

That means you.

TREVOR. NORTHANGER ABBEY! YES.

CHARLOTTE.	JESSICA.
Hey!	Yeah, that was a little gift for you.

JESSICA. And anyway, *P&P*, *Persuasion*, potayto potahto.

CHARLOTTE. Well, I wouldn't go that / far—

JESSICA. Tomayto tomahto.

CHARLOTTE. No, that's the opposite of my point! Focus!

JESSICA. Your point, Chuck, is that we are very different. We have different values and love different books and see ourselves in different stories, but we have earned enough self-knowledge to recognize how much better our lives are with the other one in it, even if you are a contrary snob.

CHARLOTTE. And even if you are an unrepentant populist.

JESSICA. Even if. Or because of.

TREVOR. *(Gasps.)* Like Jane's heroines! The self-discovery/ good partnership thing!

CHARLOTTE.	JESSICA.
Trevor! Nailed it!	Aw, Sweet Cheeks!

(They motion him in to join a group hug, which he does. Is this the end of the play? ...

not quite! A gentle false ending – long enough for the impulse to clap, not so long they're mad that they clapped.)

Scene Twelve
(A/K/A The Epilogue)

(**CHARLOTTE** *enters, rolling a dressmaker's dummy. It is bare. She leaves and returns with a basket of fabric scraps – multi-colored, multi-textured but also a lot of muslin pieces.* **CHARLOTTE** *begins sorting through the fabric.* **JESSICA** *appears, looking ready to leave for the night.*)

JESSICA. Chuck. What are you doing? We can go home now. Or get some wine. We hugged. They clapped. It's all good now. *(Looks around at audience.)* What are you all still doing here?

CHARLOTTE. Just playing. I found her [in the basement]. I just thought she looked a little sad. Maybe I'd dress her up a little. She seems cold. Lonely.

JESSICA. That she does. Let me help?

CHARLOTTE. Please.

(*They sort through the fabric. Slowly throughout, the two women, somewhat absent-mindedly but in that cool magical theater way, find a way to dress the mannequin. As they dress her, it slowly becomes clear that the pieces are combining to become a Regency-era dress and bonnet.*)

(After some silence.) "We live at home, quiet, confined, and our feelings prey upon us."

JESSICA. What's that?

CHARLOTTE. *Persuasion.* As usual. I dunno – I'm just thinking about Jane. Quiet, confined, but also bursting with genius and life. Do you think she had any idea that one day two dopes would be so obsessed with her that we'd do...all this?

JESSICA. Hopefully three dopes. I think we got Trevor.

CHARLOTTE. I think so too.

Do you think she'd be happy? With us, I mean?

JESSICA. I do. I think, anyway. I think she'd be psyched her stories and the women in them are still so loved. She couldn't have the fame in her lifetime, but now we're here, talking about her words and her characters –

CHARLOTTE. And her boobs.

JESSICA. Yup.

But yeah. She probably didn't see all this coming.

CHARLOTTE. Right? She couldn't have. And it keeps me coming back to Anne Elliot. Standing alone, in her super romantic Regency get-up, never expecting her life to change.

JESSICA. Is that it, Chuck? That she didn't expect anything?

CHARLOTTE. I think so. She expected to be alone. After refusing Wentworth she could expect nothing more – and her father needed so much attention.

JESSICA. Gah. He's the worst.

> *(Beat.)*

Didn't you have a whole extravaganza planned for *Persuasion*? Why didn't you do it?

CHARLOTTE. *(Shrugs.)* Oh, I don't know. It was enough for me to tell everyone why it means so much to me. That was enough.

> *(At this point, the women have sorted the fabric and some random pieces might be draped on the mannequin when…)*

JESSICA. Hey, Chuck. You notice something weird about these fabric pieces?

CHARLOTTE. What?

JESSICA. They seem to have words…on them? You see that?

CHARLOTTE. Words?

JESSICA. Yeah! Writing. Tiny, tiny writing. You see?

CHARLOTTE. My god. I do. *(Holds up a piece.)* "Let us never underestimate the power of a well-written letter." That's from *Persuasion.*

> *(**JESSICA** and **CHARLOTTE** exchange a look and **CHARLOTTE** places the piece on the mannequin. It's a perfect fit. From here on out, the lines/draping gets faster.)*

JESSICA. "She had been forced into prudence in her youth, she learned romance as she grew older: the natural sequel of an unnatural beginning." Chuck. That's *Persuasion* too.

> *(Dresses mannequin.)*

CHARLOTTE. "Anne hoped she had outlived the age of blushing; but the age of emotion she certainly had not."

> *(Dresses mannequin.)*

JESSICA. "Dare not say that man forgets sooner than woman, that his love has an earlier death."

> *(Dresses mannequin.)*

CHARLOTTE. "Now they were strangers; worse than strangers, they could never become acquainted."

> *(Dresses mannequin.)*

JESSICA. "His cold politeness, his ceremonious grace, were worse than anything."

> *(Dresses mannequin.)*

CHARLOTTE. "If there is anything disagreeable going on, men are always sure to get out of it."

> *(Dresses mannequin.)*

JESSICA. Amen. "Men have had every advantage of us, in telling their own story. Education has been this in so much higher a degree; the pen has been in their hands."

(Dresses mannequin.)

CHARLOTTE. Double amen. "I am not fond of the idea of my shrubberies being always approachable."

(Pause.)

No.

(Drops that one back into the basket.)

JESSICA. "There could have been no two hearts so open, no tastes so similar, no feelings so in unison, no countenances so beloved."

(Dresses mannequin.)

CHARLOTTE. "Too good, too excellent creature!"

*(Dresses mannequin. They place this final piece on the mannequin as **TREVOR** enters, carrying a copy of the book.)*

TREVOR. "You pierce my soul. I am half agony, half hope. Tell me not that I am too late, that such precious feelings are gone forever. I offer myself again with a heart even more your own than when you almost broke it, eight and a half years ago. Dare not say that man forgets sooner than woman, that his love has an earlier death. I have loved none but you." You guys? I get it. I really get it now.

JESSICA. Bless.

CHARLOTTE. Oh, Jane.

(They all step back to admire the fully dressed mannequin.)

The End

www.ingramcontent.com/pod-product-compliance
Lightning Source LLC
Chambersburg PA
CBHW070353120726
47909CB00008B/2831